D0598553

Rosa's Big Bridge Experiment

Sniff!
Sniff!

Child's Play (International) Ltd
Ashworth Rd, Bridgemead, Swindon SN5 7YD, UK
Swindon   Auburn ME   Sydney
ISBN 978-1-78628-557-7   L130820RW10205577
© 2020 Child's Play (International) Ltd
Printed in Heshan, China
1 3 5 7 9 10 8 6 4 2
www.childs-play.com

"Look!" exclaims Rosa. "I've built a bridge!"
"A bridge connects two places together,"
says Roman.

"Look at this!" exclaims Gina.
"I've built another bridge!"
"Ha ha! I think that's called a tunnel,"
laughs Mali.

"Let's build a bridge across this stream for our vehicles," suggests Gina.
"What kind of bridge shall we build?" asks Mali.

"The water's moving fast," says Rosa.
"And it's cold," laughs Roman.

Yap! Yap!

"The bridge has to span the width of the stream," says Rosa. "How wide is it?" "I'll measure with my net," replies Roman.

"I've made a suspension bridge," says Gina.
"It's too wobbly!" Rosa laughs.

"Sand is made of tiny particles of rock, so it should be very strong. What about an arch bridge?" asks Mali.
"Well that didn't work!" says Roman.

"The bridge has to be stable to carry any weight," explains Mali.
"What about this bat?" asks Rosa.

"We could build a bridge at the edge of the water," says Rosa. "But will it get washed away?"
"Like my flip-flop!" giggles Gina.

Swish!

"That's no good," says Gina. "The water has washed away the sand and now the bat is floating away!"

"We can balance the wood on the buckets," says Roman.
"Let's test it out!" says Rosa.

"Oh no, Snowy Dog is stuck!" shouts Rosa. "Let's build a bridge and rescue him!" suggests Mali.

Yap! Yap!

"Quick!" exclaims Rosa. "Emergency!"
"These big rocks should support
our weight," says Mali.

"What else can we use?" asks Rosa.
"This plank should be long enough
to reach Snowy Dog," says Roman.

"To the rescue!" laughs Mali.
"These stepping stones make
a great bridge!" exclaims Gina.

"Oh, Snowy Dog," smiles Roman.
"You're safe now!"
"Teamwork!" shouts Rosa.